Nile Night
Remembered Texts from the Deep

By Ione

DEEP
listening®
Institute Ltd

Nile Night
By Ione

Cover Design and CD Art: Nico Bovoso
Editing and Page Design: Marc Jensen
Author Photo: Rachel Leah Koenig
Mena House and Felluca Photos, Egypt, 1997: Maggie Kress
Ione and Pauline Oliveros, Kanazawa, Japan, 2005: Heroku Ikeda

ISBN: 1-889471-12-7

Deep Listening Publications
PO Box 1956
Kingston,NY 12402
www.deeplistening.org
Telephone (845) 338-5984
Fax (845) 338-5986
<dlc@deeplistening.org>

For Lelia Frances Whipper Ford – Inspiration for a Life

"Ione carries us in her pocket as she travels, sharing the intimate moments of her subtle, clear awareness. Her love and delight in the many-faceted experience carry us beyond imagination, underneath memory, inside feeling. Her words are an exquisite boat carrying us out on the true, deep waters."

- Andrea Goodman

"'Nile Night: Remembered Texts from the Deep' will move your mind with sounds, sensations and feelings; arousing your dreams and taking you far into that fabled land of Egypt. How fortunate for me that I shared one of these journeys with Ione and can find my own memories amplified as I dive into the depths of these writings. What an enrichment to have these poetic texts and to keep them close for reference. Ione will take you along with her and also give you space for yourself as you connect with these beautifully nuanced words."

- Pauline Oliveros

"When the Nile floods the land, all Egypt turns into a kind of sea. Only the cities remain above water like the Aegean Islands. At such times, ships no longer keep the course of the river bed, but sail right across the plain."

Herodotus of Halicarnassus (484 BC - 425 BC)

Foreword

Nile Night... Only the title, yet I feel myself immediately slipping into trance, into dream, falling through time/space into the collective. *Remembered Texts from the Deep.* "Remembered Texts," these words resonate, startle me, awaken my intention—yes, she is right, I must *Remember... from the Deep.* I slip back, out of logic, "this is night river shine," she reminds me, "This is Nile Night." I relax again, slip deeper.

> We have been and will be on this night water
> without end
> always headed back/always headed out...

There is no reason to hurry. I can savor this journey that, with each image, becomes more numinous. Ione's language is beyond imagism. The psyche, relaxed by her trance rhythms, receives the words directly as one would the pictographic writings of ancient cultures. Her images, like the hieroglyphs which drift in and out of these texts, are sacred, and as such convey powerful subtleties, subtleties capable of transmitting healing vibration. And there is a mastery, within which, I relax further.

Deceptively simple moments, such as *Philae Preparation List*, become intimate windows into active pilgrimage. Realizing we are not left out of this journey, we sense, with great anticipation, that living ritual is about to occur. We witness the question what is *essential?* And as in a dream we are led into the Temple, we merge with the living poet, the teacher, the healer, the guide, as she, dynamic and vast within ritual is "melting against the walls / Letting stone cushion and cradle...Pressing the hieroglyph for Energy – for Water – " This is a master who is sharing. We are embraced. She brings us in and she teaches us how to *bring it out*, through letters, lists, journals, poems, moments lived and reflected upon, moments lived again through reflection.

Moments dreamt, moments remembered, moments suspended in mystical fragment and moments fully disclosed with utterly lucid clarity. These texts are but a few of the subtle silken threads of a powerful tapestry. Illuminating threads, from a life perpetually woven, woven from the source, woven from *the Deep*, woven with the graceful, mudra-shaped fingers of compassion.

Rachel Leah Koenig
Atlantic Beach, NY

Author's Note

It happens this way during performance – texts and sounds are inspired by the moment, a moment that includes music, other performers, the surrounding environment and the audience. Sometimes already written words come through, morphing into new permutations creating an entirely spontaneous version of the original.

I have begun to capture some of these words, putting them down on paper, creating a kind of recycling of remembered texts.

Nile Night: Remembered Texts from the Deep represents a selection of these remembrances, along with other writings inspired by many numinous journeys to Egypt.

The accompanying *Nile Night* CD is a sonic trace of collaborative performances with the composer Pauline Oliveros, recorded in the azure of Cassis, France at the Camargo Foundation.

IONE
May 19, 2008
Cassis, France

Deep Listening On the Nile

Quiet after the siege of child vendors

after tea and karkadé, cokes and bright necklaces

after chatter and gossip

my hennaed hand

Shadows Listen, facing each other
facing stars, facing smooth, sliding sail

Our felucca moving across water

Squeal/creak of wood against wood

slip of chain against chain

facing night

moon Venus/ moon /Saturn

circle around, water wind lapping /Sirius
dark and shine at once make obsidian

this is night river shine

this is Nile Night

Moving swiftly now, the curve and arc of sail

in endless weddings to the dark above

Oh, we will never forget this listening

How long the shore eludes us

We have been and will be on this night water

without end

always headed back / always headed out

even as the outrageous bray of donkey

breaks the air and

Prayers float out widening from river's edge

Postings from the Edge of Dreams

Each night now,
I am once more aboard The *MS Nubian Sea*
When a call awakens me
I must reassemble myself through
8 thousand miles and 12 dimensions
from the red searing soul sand
the secrets of the pyramids
beyond the pyramids
the String Theory in action

This Death
This "us" we left behind
This Gratitude for the haunting
of my dreams

Enter: The Sound of crows
perched upon oracular pine
penetrating panes of
glass / echoing:

"Two is one / all is one
Never Forget
This!"

11 October 2001

Dashour The Red Pyramid

Going down farther
than I want to go
But we are committed to it
And continue on
Surely we will emerge again
Into the light.

Sometimes
Going up is like
Going down
Deep inside
a journey
Into the heart
of the matter

You're going where some part longs to be
While another curls up back home in bed.
This is where they told you not to go
Old hands caress still on these walls
Fingertips smoothing
what's close to forever
Touching yours

You were, you know
You were born for this
Undeniable stone rising

9 • Nile Night

Yes this is your breath
Yes, pulling you on
To this place beyond stars
Where you no longer are
And you know nothing.

Abu Simbel Two Temples
THE GREAT & THE SMALL
2000

For Paulette and Alex

Our boat steadily approaches – the two flags waving and whipping in the wind in front of the prow. On and on we flow over the rippling waters of the Nubian Sea. Which hill, which ridge, far in the distance will emerge as the great sculptures of Ramses? Always seen from the air, never from this vantage point. Ramses.

All the boat passengers mill about, some never glimpsed before. Where have they been hiding? Where have we been hiding? Now in new relationship to each other we are all up on deck fully visible in a new way. We – they pull out binoculars, stake out places at the railing – settle onto lounge chairs, speak to each other quietly but with an intensity that bespeaks the mounting anticipation.

We come closer in – finally getting the true scope of it, seeing the tiny ant tourists (us two years before). They are bedazzled by sun and sheer rock grandeur, dwarfed by the immensity of the stone.

Now we are finally pulled in along the dock, watching the prowess of the sailors, their nimble maneuvers – these same ones who a few nights ago while the boat rose in the dark-

ness beside them, sat on the nearby rocks smoking sweet to-
bacco with their hookahs. Now one scrambles up; and un-
furling the heavy rope begins to attach the boat to preset
stakes in the rocks.

A few moments later, the boat still, I sit in the upper lounge
talking with a friend, my back to the temple shore.

"These temples faced a sacred vista," our guide, Sohaila's
words echo in my ears, "But we don't know what it was."

The light shifts, slips a notch, and before my eyes, across the
way the slanting sun etches a clearly delineated line of pyramids into the mountain face. And for a few moments I
know what it was. I know what they knew.

That night we slip onto shore, and enter the temples for the
first time without hoards of others pressing in. A shadow of
the way we might have seen them millennia past, without
the hot sun stamping us down into the dirt.

Here are details of the army camp of Ramses – The beauty
of Het Hert and the Nubian Neterw, Satet and Annukis,
Khnum.

The smaller temple is for Nefertari, the Nubian beauty who
was beloved of Ramses, for whom he built (unheard of !)
her own temple, next to his.

Nefertari, ranking priestess of Het Hert, still reigns in here, and in the Holy of Holies, her cow face and head receive the rays of the sun, while behind the wall, the secret of the rest of her body resides.

Out front, Aida scratches into the night – emerald mint liqueur is served in little plastic cups. Someone has thought to take care of us on this journey. One of us is kissed in the dark. And one of us will listen to Aida in his room for weeks afterward.

Amada- Old Nubia

Mirage

Our big boat takes us on the great lake beyond the dam,
viewing temples retrieved from the rising waters
– a prayer for those still beneath the silken water –
for those dispersed from home forever

From blues, from deep red earth, from sacred carvings

On the shore, trudging toward a rising
temple in the sand,
we leave the blue galabayed guard

to his pet scorpions, watching as our sneakered feet

make new mystery markings in the sand

A smiling waiter appears in the midst of the desert
to offer cool lemonade.

We drink.

Mirage.

Why?

Why do you want to go up there?
There's nothing up there, said
Ali's brother at the barbeque
In the proverbial shadow of the Great Pyramid

Then he asked me to accompany him a few short steps away
from the gathered guests
"I think I love you," he whispered, urgently.
"Thank you," I replied.

Ferry Across the Nile

Leaving the others at the dinner table, I walk through the
lobby and out into the night.
Heading down to the dock. I have heard in these new times
of cell phone availability in Egypt that Pauline is coming.

She has made the plane to Aswan
She has made the ferry to the Hotel.
She is on the ferry.

Small groups gathered in the dusk waiting.
Palms and flowers and soft scents – the glistening lights
across on the water.
I can see the small boat arriving, an important fan of water
behind it.
Shadowy figures on board. Someone is waving –
I wave back.

As it gets closer, I see that the one waving is not Pauline
She is sitting on the other side, smiling, now waving.
Here, I am here! Everything in me is saying
I am on the dock
You are arriving.

Stand Here

Stand here, they told me and she will come
5 years old at the camp for older girls,
I waited as they said
at the end of the dusty road
And then the miracle –
the tiny silhouette in the distance
Her picture hat –
Her long dark hair
My mother.

Philae Preparation List

White
Release / Seed
Introspection / prayer
Bring a vision or image
as offering

Thunder's Attendants
Lorah and Roz
Incense / Sage lighting

Initiation Notes
Philae Temple 1997

It is the willingness to be
Perfectly in the moment.
And then the ability to be open
While being perfectly in the moment.
One or more people who do this
Can allow it to happen for others.

This is the function of a priestess.

There is the osmosis of Hieroglyphs,
Meaning seeping in.
They are sacred!
Magical in themselves.

We are being worked
By their magic
More and more
As we open to it.

Keep recreating it.
Double tracking it.

Holding the space/authority
The temple recreates itself.
The priestesses are still alive.
The wisdom is still here.

All that is happening now
Is known in the past.

This is the downtime
Of the sacred wisdom
The conscious obliteration
Of hieroglyphs.

A Message from Imhotep
Holy of Holies – Philae

For Thunder

Dear One,
You are the Five Gold Star – Venus
The mystery – the child lives
Woman child / child woman
Woman births the girl child
Parthenogenesis

The Little Room

The Nubian guide
I've known forever
has taken my hand,
his – large and soft and dry
Encompassing mine
Leading me here
To safety

Temple birds are singing
full throated
as we white birds gather inside

I am melting against the walls
Letting stone cushion and cradle me.
Pressing the hieroglyph for
Energy – for Water –
I bring a message for each

The Temple of Luxor

At night, of course.
This year the white owl who lives atop the first pylon
Has a baby.
We see them both and
Recognize the baby by its flighty
boldness.

A Letter to Thunder

Dear Thunder,

*Here's a text I wrote for the members of the recent journey-
I thought I'd share it with you.*

Remembering all of you with fondness, still floating on deck
on the Nile – where else to be in this life or any other?

Remembering Sohaila's powerful tears of greeting,
and still feeling the greatness of the great pyramid
emanating its ancient secret message.

Being nestled between the paws of the Sphinx!

The sanctity of sitting with Sekhmet.

Her smile at being anointed.

The Dance at Karnac and Thunder's wonderful directing,

The kind and gentle waiters on the boat.

The fun dancing and the wonder of Thunder's "Cher Moment"!

The food!

The Singing in the Temple of Denderah – that seemed to
transcend ages, vibrating our message of peace to the stars.

The sacred ceremonies, and the privilege of being with each
of you in quiet and private moments as well as in the group.

The sacred shopping.

The white owls at Karnac, on the Nile, and at Luxor Temple.

Nathaniel's wonderful spirit – and his bouncing out with the spoon during the musical spoons game.

Nathaniel's beginning to teach us about the hieroglyphs at Denderah and the other temples.

The depth of Abydos and sacred ceremony.

The cry of the water buffalo outside after the ceremony.

The guard who knew Om Seti

The guard who held our hands and then protected Andrea and me from intruders at Philae.

The one who kept saying Happy New Year!

The beauty of the scarves catching the gentle breeze in the pipe ceremony on the terrace.

The expressions of wonder and pleasure on the Egyptian faces as they watched us – and later spoke with us.

The families, the friendship.

The camels and the camel riders, the donkeys braying.

THE SUFI DANCER!

He is still spinning, I know it: whirling, red, yellow, gold and

brown, a prayer in movement.
We all slip back in now and sit with him, letting the music,
the reality beyond reality carry us along with the dance.

He'll always be there and we'll always be right there with
him.

Wonderful Sohaila!

Driving along behind, beside and in front of our bus as we
headed to the airport for the return flight.

Jesse's hilarious tour guide monologue along the way, that
made us laugh through the sadness of departure.

The softness on the landing of our plane on our return to
Kennedy.

Hotep!

From IONE
2003

The Overseer

We pass by, my brother, Guy and I –
We've been walking around this Bent Pyramid,
feet dusty in the sand, sun beating down when we come across them.
Workers lined up beside each other, strung along a gentle slope,
patiently removing the earth in baskets, carrying them up to be dumped behind a piled high mound of stone and sand.

One tall and weathered man in soft wrapped turban wants to speak with us.
We shy away.
"No baksheesh!" Guy says to me, shaking his head.
We've had enough.

I silently agree – Keep on walking.

But the man is standing in his full dignity.
We've erred in our judgment. It's clear to us even before he speaks.

"No Baksheesh!" he calls out, as we approach him slowly.
"Ha!" he is half talking to himself, half muttering,
"I could give you Baksheesh-"

"Where are you from?" he wants to know, surveying us

with narrowed eyes.
Just wants to talk.

"Ah, yes, New York, California..."
He knows of these places –

"Here," he gestures, "there is a German team excavating the causeway of this pyramid."

Yes, ah yes, a German team...

Gruffly, he yells in Arabic at one of the men who is slacking off behind him, and we begin to take our leave,

"It was good to talk with you," we call back.

"Thank you!"

On schedule, we're heading back to our bus, unexcavated conversations pile up like sand dunes in our minds.

Months later I see him again. I am lying in bed watching the Discovery Channel.

I'm delighted! I'm back in Egypt again and he is the Over-seer of the workmen on another important dig –

The search for Imhotep, my guide.

May, 2001

At the Locks of Esna

2003

Several women are sounding in a circle at the center of the lounge when the vendors arrive at the sides of our boat, the *SS Intrepid.*

Helloo-ooo! Hell-ooo!

Hell-o-o!
Turning away from Andrea's class, I rush to the porthole, sticking my head out just as a busy sailor passes.

Out there, beyond the railing, little boats are bobbing on the black glistening water. Their hulls are filled with packages of goods. Young brown boys in worn galabeyas hold up Nefertiti, King Tut and Cleopatra table cloths. Thin and muscular, they balance themselves easily, already tossing wrapped up packages to the big boat next to us. She is *The Egyptian Miss.*

This is when I decide to begin a list of the names of boats that float past us on the Nile, the way I once did with French Cafés. Café Terminus, Café du Cinema....

Nubian Sea
Miss Egypt
Nile Treaure

Kasr El Nil
Beau Rivages
Seti I
Sudan
Solitaire
Salacia
Grand Princess
Hurmia
Glory
Calamera Mirage I
Royal Boat
Miriam
Nile Ruby
Nile Dream
HS Radamis
Nile Symphony
The World
Police
Napoleon
Orchid
MS Miss World
Star Of Luxor
MS Beau Soleil
Nile Legend
Anni
Rosetta
M/S Savoy
Nile Bride
Vittoria
Re`ve du Nil

Down in my cabin once more, I pull the curtains and peer into the night. Shore lights and stars in familiar constellations: Orion, Sirius.

I recall ancient words: *The earth is a reflection of the heavens.*

We are docked prow first against a gravel bank – in line with several of the other boats for passing through the locks. We are all close now – clearly of the same family. Somewhere – at a distance now –

plaintive, hopeful, insistent:

"Hell-ooo!"

Café De L'Avenir

She would shuffle the names of cafés and bars on her little table like tarot cards, each with its story and symbols, each with its portents: *Restaurant Bar le Mistral, Café Au Depart, Café au Petit Relais, Aux Rendezvous des Postiers, Café de la Gare, Café Terminus...*

Then she'd leave a message for him to meet her at one of the cafés, depending on her mood. So there was the *Café de L'Avenir* with its white tables out front on an angle to the street and above it the *Hotel de L'Avenir* where the future was promised with each demi, each sleep, each dream. They loved to talk about taking a room and making love upstairs.

When she was feeling nostalgic for the country, her house in the South, she would send a message by the neighbor's son. Would he please meet her at 6:30PM at the *Coucher du Soleil Café?* She found it was impossible to think about her house there and at that hour. It was always most crowded then and she enjoyed the hoards pressing by on their way from work.

Once he called and said he'd found a wonderful place for her, the worst café in Paris: the *Café du Cinema.* They looked in vain for a movie theater nearby. The waiter, when questioned, replied with a shrug. Upstairs, the *Hotel du Cinema* tempted them, but as usual, only in conversation, in fantasy.

Finally they decided that it was named after the French expression he liked best, "Ça c'est du cinema!

Oh, yeah, it's just like the movies. A farce in other words, a noisy farce... comically or perhaps even tragically unreal.

They sat shouting to each other as the cars and trucks rumbled by, frenetic Paris drivers maneuvered dangerously close to the curb a few feet away from their table. Soot landed in their beer. Fumes made them cough, their noses tickled.

She reached into her bag for tissues.

Inside two men were playing the pinball machine. Its dings and ch-dings issued faintly out. The woman behind the bar returned her glance non-commitally, as though to assure her that she didn't care who she was or why she was there, or if she ever came back to the café again.

"It's almost exhilarating," she thought, "It almost makes me feel good!'

Moon, Mond, Luna, Lune

Remember my name

I am old one, *L'ancienne, Lantepasada, Abuela de tus sueños*
You remember – the old house
and I am calling, calling,
but you can't find the path

I return again. Now here

I am moon-mother, moon-daughter, moon-child.
Your light, your window in time, silver egg born from the
néant

Something out of nothing

I am *Sina* pounding grain, my daughter by my side. I am the
horned lady, *Het Hert, Hathor*, Heavenly Cow. I am rouge,
noire, *blanche*.

See me, I am *Om Tara Tu Tare Ture Swaha*!

I come down to answer your call. I am winged *Nut*, *Nek-
hbet* the Sacred Vulture, I wear the feather of *Maåt*.
I am the feast of light in a sea of tranquility.

Remember, I am *Auset* shining. *Isis* in flames. Woman of
flame and water, wild one. *Ceridwen*

Night Horse.

I am changing! I am Io Sounding. Hear the bees in my hair?
I am *Soma, Chango, al Lat, Hina, Chnadra, Mama Quili,
Akua BU.* Lions pull my chariot across the night, swallowed
by sweet *Nut.*

The stars are my lovers, Innana above and below.

Orange of *Sekhmet* roaring.

Listen, I am the milk of your dreams flowing through all
time. *Lait primordial –*
Mother is here –
Open your mouth,
Drink me in.

Take this path toward shore. We ride this wave home.

*Invocation sent to the surface of the Moon in St. Paulten,
Austria 1999 as a part of Pauline Oliveros' composition
"Echoes From the Moon"*

Post from the Isle of Crete

Viewing Andrea's post, I must comment upon how Pauline and I sat upon the spacious 2nd floor terrace of our room in Crete overlooking the gardens and the pool, and in the short distance the cerulean sea (Aegean, I think – we'd better all look at a map!) Ionian we cross on the way to Egypt. Anyway, we had a great Greek Salad and some sparkling water and our feet were up and we were inhaling the sea and its color, just taking it in, when they – Andrea, Ka Sha and Monique bringing up the rear – the three graces, towel wrapped and wet, gleaming and smiling and laughing approached on the path beneath us. They'd just been in the water and were ecstatic. I became ecstatic seeing them. They are happy! They are happy! I exclaimed to Pauline – and later wrote in my journal. For this alone it is all worth while.

They looked like dolphins all three, and like the great mother in all her magnificence the threefold one.

Love, IO

The Labyrinth

We wound our way back from the farthest reaches
of upper Egypt
sailing into ancient Khmet – touching ground in lower Nubia
braving the surly Temple guards of Kalabsha Temple
Two priestesses locked in the tower
released by the timeless sound of distress
footsteps over steep red sand, the heat in our hearts
Kisses on our lips
Secret stairways and soundings into the well of wailing
Trailing through corridors and waiting rooms,
the terminals of refugees between the realms
Circling in the buses of our transport
and one lost passport,
the missing papers of desire
for the sweet madness of Cairo,
the depth of our longing
skirts sweeping through the marbled lobbies,
veiled women and sheiks,
bombs and riots on CNN
Another loop and we circle through Athens
listening for the stilled voices of the Acropolis
We heard them singing from the island
at the Palace of Knossos where the living Minotaur awaits:
Evangelos, who carries the string, guide to his own maze –
A man with sons, like us, a man in love with terraces and
pillars, the abodes of kings, the apartments of the queen –

We saw her there, brushing her hair, in a trance, dreaming
of the great wild beast and the taste of tart honey
While below, Theseus dances with bulls and
maidens leap across the Horns of the Goddess.
The Minotaur loves the travails of sons,
the courage of women,
These wide eyed ones, proud of their breasts,
of their fertility
touching heart and commanding listening, he speaks in front
of the frieze of three in curls,
noses and chins in charming defiance
"One day, I was guide to a group of women who came to
the island on a boat – they loved this frieze – they were all
women in relationships with each other. I believe, I believe
I can speak freely of this among us.
"I believe that these women loved women, not so much because of sex, but because of – what is the word – yes, it is
partnership. Because of the *partnership.*"

Later, partners sitting
on a terrace between the Ionian and the Aegean
Watch Three Priestesses dipping in the Sea of Crete
braced by the cold and laughter
blessed by the love of water
The Monster is appeased,
The Mother is happy

Lord Kitchener smiles

Lord Kitchener smiles and takes another sip of

Karkadé

His cup is from the finest

China

All is right with the world

He is the center

of the merry-go-round

Off stage carousel horses

Champing at their bits

Laugh

They are pulling the circle

round and round

Elephants shuffling

step by step

side by side

Skin to skin

Speaking in code

Listening through their feet

for the sounds of their family

Not so far away

"We are here, we are safe

We will survive this..."

The heavy laden island

breathes

a sigh of relief

Palm fronds brushing

Magnolias straining each to each

Vying for their scents

Bougainvilleas /Jasmine

Clematis / Hibiscus

Crying sweet smells of intimacy

This, their endless war

The boat man awaits Lord Kitchener

in the dark

While back across the water

At the Winter Palace

A woman in white approaches her

Long mirror

A small box on a low table

Opens to reveal one tiny mirror
And another

There is no turning back from

Her journey

Lord Kitchener sets forth

Across the black river

A seed from each variety

Sinks lower into moist soil

The flowering island

Breathes a sigh

of acceptance

"We will survive this…"

Kitchener, Ontario 2006

On the Rondout

This morning the seagulls skate over thin ice,
Skirting black water deep beneath –
Pools of shine against a dusted white cover –
Algae and old leaves lurking

My crumbs fly high
and scatter, landing softly

The heralds sound the cry,
Etching fine lines
As they skid to position nearby.
Eyes on me as sharp as needles
Since a half mile back.

The ducks, just a few –
slower but very interested,
coming in fast as they can –

No way to catch up a piece of Chinese crackle
before a white gull – just no way.

It's useless to try and favor them
though they try without conviction –
to be a presence in the pecking order.

And then as if with trumpets blaring,

The swans round the big moored boat,
Coming in from the river
They've heard the fuss.
They want in.

I rush to meet them and they disappear.
Ducking under the dock, they emerge again.
Just a bit left, thank heavens
For these two old friends.
They gobble up old,
Healthy protein crackers with gusto.

That's it! I declare and begin my way back
Turning every now and then to see.

The gulls don't go near the long necked couple,
king and queen of this morning's catch,
But the ducks go close,
Receiving a few vigorous pecks
For their trouble.

On the way to Kanazawa

We've been traveling 8 1/2 hours.
Flying at 35,000 feet

Our shadow is a ball of light
On the frozen ground below
Black abyss – obsidian river

Crackling, frozen tundra
Speckled-white on white

Dappled shades
Secrets of a continent of ice

Frozen peaks in hieroglyphic time
Flow edges

We are crossing the International Date Line

Siberia
To the right on our map:

Gulf of Shelokesa
Sea of Okhotsk

3 1/2 hours more to go.
A specter
A will o' the wisp
A window in no time

Drifting now,
Over dense cumulus clouds,
Our light continues on.

November 1, 2006

Hidden Forest

Night and this Forest Path
Dreams me
To the
Place of being

I know you
Now
Remembering
These lights
These trees in late summer shadow

Voices rising in night

Knowing you

These are the important ones
The forgotten dreams that haunt us still

I am listening for you
In night

Forgiveness
Candles and laughter in the dark

Les Cérisiers

And the taste of butter
Steeped so slowly

Wine and the Gypsy dancing on the table
Music curling round her skirts in soft smoke

Notions, motions

The author of cities is gone, but not that long ago
Wait. A traveler passes this way

Divine architect

His name
Inscribed on each leaf
We all danced here a few years ago

A child sits on the lower branch of the tree
Acrid scent of Gitanes

This music
This night
Dreams me

For Elaine Summers' Hidden Forest
Lincoln Center, Damrosch Park
August 23, 2007

Remembered Text

Remember when forgiveness
Was only a word

It had nothing to do with

You

You did not know
That you would

Need it

That you would
Crave It

That you would
Be it

Your heart in flames

Like a bird

Falling

I won't go out again
The neighbors can wait to see me

Inside I have light
I have Illumination

Downstairs on the first floor, the birds fly free,
Swirling round
In the upper floor there are the bees
Buzzing

Outside, a giant wing stretches upward to the second floor

It is my sorrow that burns you

So many of them come out of the woods now, you can see
them drifting across the field.

We sat one day
In the circle, doing the dance

Open, open, open
Free the bird

Thaw the frozen hawk

Six For New Time

For Pauline

Says the Ouiji Board,

"Life is not the chair,
Life is Sitting."

One Life

this one
and
this one
and
this one
and
this one
and
this one
and
this one

The Queen Approaches Her Throne
Wind over water

Hell's Angels in a Pink Van

Escape from Concentration

"Our thoughts are Time...."
Time
Being
Being
Time

2.

The Warrior stops to sip
the potion of the Gods

White Crows Rising in the night
Beyond the temple grounds

Escape from concentration
The King comes to have a home

One sound fills the sky

One Sound
One Sound
One Sound

this one
and
this one
and
this one
and
this one
and
this one
"Life is not the chair
Life is Sitting."

Good fortune
No time
Time
Being
Being
Time

1999

What Happens When You Die

While you travel in another dimension
Your mail keeps coming to those you left behind
with "special offers."

Dear Daddy:

Ash Wednesday in your 88th year.

This new moon, tracks my feet upon the path.
Feu d'artifice in the night announce your taking leave,

et l'hibou de Chambourcy...

I had to relinquish your body to strangers
Who became my intimates

"Everything that takes form one day fades away,"
said the Buddha.

We practice knowing this and

Remembering that nothing ever leaves us.

We are still at dinner on the terrace,

still savoring the hand of bridge,
the view from the dining room window
looking into infinity,

full of joys and complaints,
pain and good wine, champagne with friends,
our papers all about,

the radio on in the other room
even while the hurricane circles 'round.

Dear Daddy:

You and the great trees of Versailles
up-rooted this year by a great storm

The likes of which we've never seen

Read on the occasion of the cremation of Dr. Hylan Garnet Lewis on March 13, 2000 at Mt St. Valerian, Nanterre France.

For Maggie

1.

As near as your heart can stand it
Can accept its existence

Without expanding beyond itself
Into Light

You
sending me off into rainbows and

Giant Taras made of cumulus clouds
You
turning away
You
beside me

Your rabbit, your dog

Your cat

Though blind can see

Your departure

Accompanies you through darkness

You

A belly dancer
These coins jangle at your belly

A monk sits in a Sacred Cave

A carpet, a chair and neighbors
Chanting

A Teacher prepares to move into
Final meditation

The Sacred land awaits
Not far from here

Not so far after all.

2.

Off the islands
She waits in profound waters

These dreams of thousands of years

Remembers

These stories from the depths

Accompanies these boats to land

These Ancestors ride

The space between you and me

With your dark eye

An ancient coin of life
Turning to surf the waves

Traveling onto black sand

Here it takes two days for dreams to arrive,

Rushing across waters and over vast terrains

Here I am taking the train, feeling its metal flank

Leaving the suitcase at the other end

I get on

Traveling internally to reach it

Getting off again

Moving through sleek dining cars

Comfortable passengers

No time
Must find the suitcase

Can you describe it?
Is it the black one, the purple one, the long one?

Inside the house
The old apartment
At 45 East
The living room
There is an old lover
Arriving
To discuss with you
To receive a token a remembrance
of time long past and yet ongoing

Eternal as passion sparks in the simple embrace.
Ah yes

That's what it was, that's what it is.

But I'm still trying to get to you
A graphic, a pyramidal shape, a silver obelisk

This must be pointing the direction
To you
On your swift Journey
Beyond me.

À Cassis February 1, 2008

For V and J

Becoming accustomed to new ways
of being, old patterns return.

Contemplating a walk to the post office
with *Cartes Postales et timbres*

Awaiting the elixir of morning light

The mystery bird, huge in silhouette
tops a tree point beyond our
kitchen windows
has grace enough to disappear
as I rush
slowly out.

***

"The Purple heron is a likely basis
 for the Egyptian phoenix,
 bennu, which means purple heron"

Dimitris in Oz, a plaintive bird,
cries out in anxious text online:

 "Turning Mediterranean isn't it?
What next Purple Heron? Night Heron?
Squakko Heron?? Dalmation Pelican?

Are there any heronries nearby the Ibis could use??"

***

Here the sea is upside down,
we live within it curving upward from the terrace,
sighted higher than the stone pathway too,
with its pink/mauve flowers –
Someone loved planting these,
they are so content.

Dreaming beside the budding cactus
a soft pink grey cloud calico
glimpsed upon a low rooftop
rolls over and over in ecstatic delight,
thrusting paws and belly up
then pricks up ears over the foliage,
face hidden,
watching the watchers.

***

Ensconced at tiny tables, determined café sitters hover
in sunglasses and scarves, light sweaters and jackets

It is winter, after all. and though there is cachet in being
here,
l' *insouciance* of summer is far away.
These are regulars, for now at least, expats from Paris and
ailleurs
a little *apéritif au soleil* before lunch –
side-walk tables hopeful a few feet away

best settings calling out,
red tulips glimpsed *à l'intérieur*
each showing true colors, here, shades of toast,
there, deep sea blue and white, in cheerful competition
Choose me, choose me!
Soldes 50% announced by two or three boutiques
Come in and buy something now.

Further along – a part and yet *à part*
the ancient stone bench, where sunning elders
take their centuries old space

Each day there are lovers snug against the lighthouse wall,
confident of their fears
facing blank benevolence,
a smooth sea full of unseen fish

The fisherman has gone home long since.
And the mature woman and man
somewhere in their 50s, are strolling
toward their *déjeuner*

Close enough for holding hands.
"We will find a nice table," his voice a calm caress.

***

Here we are always en face du chateau
High on its promontory against Calanques

"Oh," they say, "it is all closed up."

I imagine the walkways, the stone walls rising up
completely silent, no entrance to the sea views
where marauders were suspected.

They came to every cove of course and we know now how
the *Contes de Barcelone* bestowed this region
upon their troublesome adolescent sons,
14 years old and ready for war,
getting them out of the way
to hold real power for themselves.

History rises implacably with each
step, each half memory, each half forgetting
of how things are
precarious and perilous,
of how in this film we are safely
caught between loops
of past and future.

Photographed going in backwards,

fast forward, a woman arises from the water
wearing her crown of flowers
A queen.

Yet it is not the king but the Jack who awaits her.
Ever the pretender to the throne.

This must be it, the alchemy of
the dream, the magician within the
mechanism

the immortal infant listening
to the technology of the sacred

the vibrant child in the darkened room
the mother loving in two dimensions,

his secret awakening
in the center of the camera obscura

to find the castle of the railroad King,
the father of his father
turned upside down
the lineage ever returning
to haunt and instruct
to *bouleverser* anew

to give permission
to live inside an emerald!

"The dead are alive",
a great aunt's message from long ago
and other voices open in the sky

No way to forget this
Now

Epilogue

Cairo – The Last Morning

I awaken from numerous involved dreams. Five AM wake up call. The night is luminous still, my terrace window open. The lotus shape on the iron work looks more graceful than ever.

I throw myself unwillingly into the morning and do the last packing- odds and ends- over a Turkish coffee with milk (!) that is delicious. As I watch the mist and then fog roll in with day light- covering the view- my whole life seems to rise before my eyes- moments when things went askew- I see myself from a distance from the perspective of the Nile- however and I forgive myself.

Down below the multicoloured fellucas await the day. On the bridge, pinpoints of light pierce the thickening morning mist with a warm yellow glow.

On the plane returning, my seat-mate- an Egyptian, is, I see from his landing card- going to get off in Athens. He looks out the window and I seem to sense a quiet sadness- or is he merely sleepy? My own mood is pensive.

The Mirages?

Inverted cities in the sky. Cairo is inverted in my mind. My life inverted prismatically for me to see- cast against the vivid imagery of this country- mingling there- I watch my self- another me- perhaps the real me (my true self) disappear into the dirty crowded streets.

This night I will be with the desert again- near Saqqara. The temple dogs keep their distance.

I am guard tonight.

- From the First Egyptian Journal - April 12, 1983

- Remembered, April, 2008, Cassis, France

MOVING BACKWARD IN TIME

EARLY REMEMBERED TEXTS

The First Night in Aswan

Something is happening outside my window.
I awaken from a nap and pull the drapes wide.
It is the sunset. It takes hours to go down, raspberry
To black raspberry along the hills in front of me.

On the Nile, fellucas glide across the mauve reflection
of the sky.
Suddenly a flock of silver Ibis birds
Moves in swift formation, rippling upward.
The chant from a nearby mosque follows them across the
water.
And the birds rise, becoming little white
Pinpoints, then veils of clouds beside the bright
And steady planet Venus which chooses this moment to
Begin to shine.

On the morning I bought your beads
I climbed upward toward the final resting place
Of the Aga Khan.
"Nubian, Nubian...", whispered
the felluca boatmen crouched at the water's edge.
Camels braying, ducks quacking, tourists chattering
The road up to the Aga Khan's is steep, hot and dry.
It was enough to buy your scented beads in the cool
Shade of the flowering trees, call Sika from his
Breakfast and set sail on the river again.

Gift in Upper Egypt

In the night the flower smell overwhelms
Strolling guests on the pathway leading up
to the hotel. Stunned, I stop to find its source.
From the darkness a turbaned figure in long galabaya
Steps forth.
"Here. It is here," he beckons.

As I approach, he hands me honeysuckle and points to the
heavy laden tree above him
I thank him profusely and wander down the path.

Then when I am just beyond the turning point.
His voice questions, softly,
"Baksheesh? Baksheesh?"

On the straight arrow highway between Cairo and
Alexandria
There are Camel Crossing signs along the way-
Shaped like camels.

Dozing in the car, I think I am thinking, then notice I am
dreaming.

It was like that on the river that day as I slumbered in the
Felluca close to the water.   I opened my eyes just in time to
see
A pack of Cleopatra cigarettes floating down the Nile.

The following are words as told to a visiting French woman by the woman called "Kuchuck Hanem":

Oh, my dear sister.... I will tell you about it!

I wasn't yet awake that morning when Said came running with the news that the *cawadja's* boat was in the harbor again. Right off I set the children to cleaning and refilling the lamps.

The village musicians had to be notified and provisions had to be ordered. I sent Naja down to tell them we'd be awaiting them that evening as the sun sets. I saw to it that this child of mine, whom that took for a girl-friend, was as tempting as could be--- though they'd not touch her!--and I let her take Beauty along as well.

They looked quite pretty setting off to the river, Naja with her long, dark newly beaded hair and my big, billowing white pants I let her wear. And Beauty, the henna-spotted sheep, of course, following behind.

"Make sure not to loosen its velvet muzzle," I cried after her.

"I am always careful!" she called back. She scarcely turned around.

I sent Zenobi for my jewelry from the safe-keeping place and managed to do something with my hair. I am still pretty enough... and with my veils and bangles... my tattoos... plenty of time to scent these smooth breasts with rose water.

When they came up the stairs, I stood at the top to welcome them. How could they resist me?

That night I did that dance with the old steps the mustached one likes so much. Said told me that they had shaved their heads and were wearing swords, playing at being sheiks. What next? I told him, if it is true, we will laugh for weeks after. And it was true!

Grandmother taught me that old dance as a child and it is she who plays the main drum beside me still, counting out the beats, almost spoiling everything with her frowns.

She doesn't hesitate to tell me right away if I've forgotten some little step or gesture. She'll even get up and start to dance to correct me.

"Leave me be!" I'll tell her right in the middle of things, but with a smile on my lips.

"Who was it made you the most famous in the land?" she

growls and I toss back, "and who is it does the dancing, old mother?"

He wanted to spend the night again, that time, even though I tried to persuade him otherwise. This one hardly slept a wink. I'd just settled into a good snore and he'd be on top of me again. My little dog didn't really like sleeping on that silk coat instead of in my bed. But at least his belly was full the next day. No more complaints.

Look sister, on my bedroom wall I've pasted this beautiful image that one of the boys brought me. It is a label from a tin. This woman's name is 'Fame', that is what is written underneath. She is passing out flowery wreaths, it is like a part of a dance I sometimes do.

Tonight I will create a new song. I already have the opening phrases... these too, I will have Naja write on the wall beside the bed.

"I have lived a thousand years, a thousand years have I lived, though I am yet unborn."

Come- let Zenobi bring you another cup of tea, and I will show you the dance!

Manuscript breaks off here. (Document found in a trunk at

a flea market near Paris in 1955- Translation by Ione)

Note: Kuchuck Hanem was a member of the Ghawazi, a collective of famous dancer-courtesans who had been exiled from Cairo a few years before to Esna. Gustave Flaubert visited with her during his tour to Egypt in 1849 and was fascinated, describing his feelings and wondering about hers in his journal as well as in correspondence with his lover the pioneering feminist writer, Louise Colet. Kuchuck did enjoy fame in her time and Colet developed her own fascination with the Esna dancer and reputedly sought her out in Egypt some years later.